1200 Miles from Los Angeles

A Novella

by Steven W. Simon

Third Edition, July 2024

ISBN: 979-8-348-48059-2

boundharepress.com

In remembrance of my grandmother
and those who were lost.

For my brothers: Benedict, Gautam,
Jake, Mikal, Patrick, and Tommy.

1998

January 4

"Let the freak get 'em," one of the girls said. Carla, I thought. She looked like the other girl. Patty. It was my first day. I knew these identical twins in high school. At first, they looked exactly alike, but after a while I could tell each right off. 'I guess it's the same when you meet a lot of new people all at once,' I thought, 'they are all identical twins.'

Carla and Patty had fake blond hair held in ponytails with scrunchies. Patty was training me. The 'freak' was a quiet girl with purple hair and almost matching purple lipstick. She had several piercings, including a hoop through her nose. I can't remember her name right now, as I write.

There were five old men waiting for a table near the host stand. One of them kept staring at Carla with a creepy grin. She smiled back with that fake smile you do when you're at work, then she pretended to busy herself behind the lunch counter. "They don't need menus," Patty said. We walked through the main dining area of the restaurant with the salad bar. The smoking section had big windows facing the gas station pumps, the street, and the highway entrance ramps.

"*The girl with the purple hair* will be right with you fellas," Patty told the four who had sat down at the booth. The other man dragged a chair from non-smoking, I still can't remember her name. He said something about the cold weather and the other men agreed. "You don't want those guys," she informed me, "they just drink coffee for hours and tip you a quarter, each one of them." She then motioned to the quiet girl. "Coffee, and don't forget that Doug gets decaf this time!"

I followed Patty back behind the lunch counter and watched the orders come up through the window that created a connection between the kitchen and the counter. One of the cooks stabbed a ticket through a metal stick and rang a bell. "Shit boy," he yelled through the window, which was really just an empty space. No one knew why they called it a 'window'. "How old are you?" I told him I was 19. "Shit, you look like you're 13 or something." I knew he was in his 50s but he looked half-dead.

A mom, dad, and their kid walked in and stood by the 'please wait to be seated' sign. They kept staring at me and I realized that I was the only one at the hostess stand. I smiled at them. I didn't know what to do. Carla said something about 'sections.' There were a lot of empty tables, would it matter if I sat them wherever? I turned around to ask the cook but he wasn't there anymore. I laughed nervously in the direction of the family then put my finger up and mouthed 'one moment.' The mom smiled at me with that fake smile that you do when you're embarrassed for someone and then she brushed the snow from her daughter's cap. The girl squirmed to remove her mother's hand.

I went to the back, behind the stoves and ovens, and found Carla smoking a cigarette at a little table. I called her Patty when I told her that people needed to be seated. She didn't correct me but kind of stuck out her chest to highlight her name tag. I felt bad.

She swore as she put out her cigarette and mumbled something about the girl with the purple hair. "If this says 'dirty' don't go in the walk-in, alright?" It was one of those magnets you put on the dishwasher so you know if the dishes are clean or dirty. I told her I wouldn't but didn't inquire further. It was my first day.

"Hi there, terribly sorry about the wait," Carla's concern was sincere. "Smoking or non?"

"Non," the mom said; I think the dad was disappointed.

Carla warned me not to go into the manager's office without knocking as we walked back to the kitchen and then scolded the purple-haired girl for not seating the family. She asked me where I was from and I told her.

"Why'd you move here?"

"My mom got a job here," I lied.

"Huh. Where's she working at?"

"I can't remember what it's called."

"You ever waited tables before?"

"No."

"Shit, my cig," she said and then went into the back. She pounded on the metal walk-in door and told Patty that she had a table and that *she* was supposed to be training me. I waited for Patty at the counter but when she came out from the back, she went straight to the family still sitting where we had left them.

"Sorry about the wait," Patty told them. She was not sincere. I walked over to the salad bar while she took their order and pushed the lettuce around with a tong. The cherry tomatoes looked weird under the fluorescent light. The purple-haired girl walked by with two coffee pots—one with a brown handle and the other was orange. I figured one was the decaf. For Doug. I watched her bend slightly into a cloud of cigarette smoke to pour the coffee and I think Doug said something about wanting Carla as a waitress next time.

The little girl wanted a strawberry milkshake. Patty ordered the purple-haired girl to make it for her. I offered to help so I could learn how. I think that offended Patty and she walked away.

I just wanted to be close enough to her to see what her name tag said. She had already told me her name, so I didn't want to ask again. Yet, once she was close to me, I was too worried that she'd think I was trying to look down her shirt. I still didn't know her name.

Two scoops of vanilla ice cream. One spoonful (the big spoon for milkshakes) of strawberries in that can of red jelly they come in. Two squeezes of the strawberry sauce. Then you put the metal cup into the mixer. Whipped cream and then more sauce. She was very nice while showing me, and she smelled as if oranges were flowers.

♦ ♦ ♦

4° Fahrenheit outside. I figure now that I'm back in my motel room, it's a good time to update my situation. My name is Sanford, I've come from Cleveland, and I intend to arrive in Los Angeles. I've made it to Nebraska. I'm stuck here.

I can't get this motel room warm. My clothes smell like the diner's kitchen. I put a towel against the bottom of the door to stop the snow that drifts through the gap. The heater makes this rattling noise so it should work. I guess it kind of works. The comforters have this weird smell, like old and sex. The faucets run brown with rust for several minutes. Everything I own is in boxes between the far wall and the one bed. Except my car. Piece of shit car.

I wonder how long I'll have to work in the restaurant until I have enough money to get it fixed. Frank, the manager, stayed in his office most of the night. He is weird. I wish I knew her name, the girl with the purple hair. She gave me ten dollars even though I'm not supposed to get any tips yet. It wasn't a 'real shift,' Frank said, that's why I didn't get a shift meal. I guess I get a free meal every time I work.

What if I had gone east instead? I could call home. No, I can't do that, not until I've made it.

It's the walk over the highway to the motel that gets me. There's nothing to contain the wind, so it breaks across my face. I had felt it when I went to my interview, but it's so much harsher after an eight-hour shift. It only snows sideways here, little frozen needles that poke into my cheeks. My eyes.

Across the street there's a building that's half convenience store and half bar. You can see into the bar side from the cash register, down a darkened hallway. In less than two years I can go in there and drink. I bought a box of Lucky Charms and a quart of milk for dinner on my way to my room.

My motel curtains are stuck closed and the walkway to the rooms has a roof with dim yellow lights hung from wires. I haven't seen the sun since I've been here. There's a man who screams at a woman, maybe she screams back but I haven't heard her. Tomorrow I'm going to start learning how to put orders into the computer for the kitchen. I don't have a spoon. Or a bowl.

Tomorrow, I will get some bowls and plates and silverware from... somewhere. And God damn it, real or not real, I'm getting my shift meal.

January 5

"Fuck Frank," Mandy whispered to me when I put my timecard into the thing to punch it. The purple-haired girl was Mandy. "You get a shift meal tonight." It was unsolicited and put me at ease. Everyone was still a twin, but less so.

I told her thanks. She smiled and I smiled and then she saw Patty and slunk away. I put on a maroon apron, the string was long and wrapped three times around my waist before I could tie it. There was already a pen in the grease-stained pocket and I found a pad with a few sheets in it and put that in the other pocket. My name tag still said 'Trainee.'

"Frank doesn't give anyone a real name tag till they've been here a week," Patty told me as I tried not to stab myself with the pin. "C'mon, we got a table. Passin' through people." I wanted to tell her that I enjoyed my first day and that she shouldn't worry about me leaving just yet but she was already at the table. I stood behind her and to the side watching. The man glanced at my name tag and nodded with a smile, as one does when they see someone uncomfortable, out of their element.

I watched her input the order into the computer. It seemed straightforward. The table number first, then there were buttons for everything we had. She showed me how to make substitutions and said that Terry, that was the cook's name, will swear at you whenever you do substitutions. I asked her how she knew they were just passing through and she told me it's because they're Black. When I didn't have much of a reaction she leaned in close to my ear.

"They're probably going to complain about something or try to get something for free and they're gonna leave a shitty tip." She straightened and her voice went back to a normal decibel, "Here's where the drinks are, unsweetened iced tea is on the first page and for some reason sweetened is on the second, it's stupid." She pressed a button, a ticket printed out and she put it on the metal carousel with little clips in the window. Terry spun the contraption and brought the ticket close to his eyes then looked through the window at the table. I think he muttered the 'n-word' but I'm not quite sure. He swore a lot on the line and smoked while he cooked. He didn't smoke at the little table in the back with the waitstaff.

The old men who drink coffee came back and insisted that Carla be their waitress tonight. Mandy told them that Carla wasn't working tonight and one of them, I think Doug who drank decaf, joked that they should get Carla's schedule. Patty pretended to puke, which I found humorous, and then told me that they don't ask for her anymore because she covers up her breasts when she waits on them. Carla used to show them off, but that was before she got quarter tips. She doesn't hide them anymore, but these old men have good memories.

Terry asked me what I wanted for my shift meal, "off the books," he emphasized. I had to look at the menu. Chicken Parmesan. I ate it at the little table in the back behind the kitchen while he stood and watched me. I offered for him to sit down with me but he didn't answer my request.

"So, who you know?" he asked me.

"Excuse me?"

"You don't know anybody, do you?"

"I know you, I guess."

"I mean from here."

"No one really, just moved here." I paused. "With my mom."

"No one just moves here."

I thought about saying, 'well *I* did,' but thought better than to be aggressive. It was my second day.

"This is really good," and I looked up at him while I chewed. "Thanks for making it for me even though, you know."

"Yeah, well, I did it to be a dick to Frank, not to do anything for you."

I pushed the plate towards the wall and dug a soft pack of Marlboro Reds out of my pocket. Terry looked at them. I saw his cigarettes yesterday, he smoked cheap cigarettes. I asked him if he wanted one and I shook the pack until a filter came out. He walked to me slowly, think a stray dog you'd just met.

"It's icy roads right now," he said as he sat down. I lit his cigarette. "That's why it's slow."

"That sucks."

"Don't matter to me, I don't live on tips." He looked at the cigarette as he exhaled the smoke. "I knew that they'd send something back."

"Who?"

"You know, *that* table." He was gauging my racism, or at least my acceptance of his own thoughts. I lit my own cigarette instead of answering. I looked at the walk-in door, it was set to 'clean.'

I asked him if there was a store where I could buy plates and he said there's a Walmart about five miles down the road.

"Anything closer?"

"I mean, there's a drugstore if you just want paper plates and stuff, they probably have that."

"How far is that?"

"About a mile from the Walmart."

Maybe the convenience store has paper plates, I thought.

♦ ♦ ♦

I fell twice on the bridge over the highway. First, I bruised my elbow, then my hip. A lone car slowed down next to me but then drove off. Maybe it's a story I'll tell to a late-night talk show host when I've made it. I wish I could drink. Mandy didn't give me any tips today, but I don't think she got enough to share.

I thought about my mother and felt guilty that I ate the chicken parmesan, treyf with its meat and dairy. I've often wondered if she keeps kosher for the religion or just because that's what grandma does.

Mandy's pretty. I've often fantasized about running away with a girl I love. Just getting into the car with whatever we have and just going. I *did* just get into the car with what I have. I *did* just go. I just forgot to bring a lover. Next time I'll plan on having the financial resources to own a better, more reliable car. I'll plan on having a lover.

January 7

Frank would always stand in the manager's office doorway when I'd come in for my shift. I always said hello and he would wave coyly before closing the door. I've yet to see him smile. Even at my interview, he kept this look like a bored dog. I remember when I shook his hand it felt oily. Not sweaty, just this weird grease that oozed from his pores and all I wanted to do was scrub my hands with antibacterial soap.

Carla's bulimic, I thought. I heard vomiting from the employee bathroom after she ate her shift meal. I've caught her in the walk-in eating sundaes and drinking milkshakes. It didn't bother me. Well, the stealing didn't; I didn't think bulimia was a good thing to have.

I should have been more cordial, more open. Even though I'd be leaving as soon as I could, I shouldn't let on.

"So you moved here cause of your mom?" Mandy asked me as she sat down at the back table. She smoked too, I guess we all did here. I told her I did move for my mom. "Is she a teacher?"

"No."

"A trucker?"

"No, she's a—" She cut me off.

"Well, that's the two choices here, unless she works at McDonald's and I'm pretty sure there's a McDonald's where you're from." She leaned in for honesty.

Her eyes were so white, so pure. I followed the brown in her irises and hoped they would lead me to reassurance that she could be trusted. That she wouldn't just go and tell Frank that I was planning on leaving as soon as I could so there'd be one less hand grasping at the meager tips.

"Why," I leaned in an inch, "is there a dishwasher magnet on the walk-in door?"

"You don't want to know."

"I do."

"Patty fucks Terry in the walk-in, so if it says 'dirty.'"

"Gross," I replied, "he's like fifty and she's like..."

"Seventeen."

"Why would she do that?"

"He pays her."

Carla yelled from the front that I had a table.

"Does Frank know that the cook is fucking a waitress in the restaurant?"

"Yeah."

"And he doesn't care?"

"He does, but Terry's his older brother and would beat the shit out of him if he said anything. I've seen him shove Frank against the wall in his office. Put a crack in the wall, still there."

I got up and served my table. They were very friendly and instead of a tip they left me a note that said Jesus loves me, but only if I love him. If not, he hates me. I went to the back, lit a cigarette, and wrote the motel name and room number on an order slip.

"If you want to hang out after your shift," I told Mandy and handed her the paper.

"That's where people get murdered."

"Oh."

"Are you going to murder me?"

"I'm more likely to be the murderee than the murderer."

She looked me over to evaluate me on this new criteria and seemed satisfied.

I watched Patty take two trips from the kitchen window to bring out an order to an obese couple. Their walkers were identical except one had rainbow streamers taped to the handles. They took to the plates with their fatty paws, ignoring the residual heat. Those are their lives, I thought, just eat, shit, sleep, repeat.

◆ ◆ ◆

There was an ambulance and two police cars in the motel parking lot when I got back tonight. A woman was handcuffed in the backseat of one of the cars. I guess she had enough. That river of deceit, of physical pain and psychological torture. I guess Mandy was right. Sometimes I'd say the Shema when an ambulance drove past, just to talk to God and remind him that I knew he was all-powerful. That he should employ mercy for whoever was in the ambulance. I didn't think it was the appropriate prayer, but it was the only one I know by heart. I didn't say it tonight.

I've barely made any money. The weather is supposed to clear up soon, maybe more people will stop for gas and decide to eat. The cold makes everything harder, makes everyone's barbs sharper. A season of suicide for boys like me. Dreamers. Idealists. Why can't I just want a steady job and a house? A wife and children? Recycling life without the

21

realization that I'm simply a cog—and cogs don't think.

They're all lawyers. Psychologists. Professors. Every related Jew. There were only two topics my grandmother would broach on our Sunday phone calls, one of which was my education. I could only feign an "it's going well." To the other query I would tell her that no, my girlfriend was not a 'nice Jewish girl.' It's both comforting and manic to be me. In this motel. In this winter.

It's getting late, I don't think Mandy is going to show up. I think I'll stop writing now.

January 8

"I thought you were maybe fucking with me," Mandy said when I opened the motel door.

"No, I wasn't." I stood there feeling the chill through my t-shirt. The winter morning sun in my eyes. "You were right, though."

"What?"

"Someone got murdered here. Last night."

"See?!"

"Or maybe not killed, maybe just hurt."

"Awesome, it's fucking cold."

I muttered an apology, let her inside and pushed the towel back against the bottom of the door.

"They're broken," I told her as she went to pull open the curtains.

"Of course, they are." She told me that if I had been staying at the Holiday Inn, she'd think I was trying to fuck her, but no one here has the confidence to fuck anyone—at least not without a transaction. And since she knew where I worked, I wasn't in a position to pay her what she's worth. Although, she added, Terry has money to fuck Patty.

"He's a cook," I explained, "he doesn't have to rely on tips."

She sat down on the bed closest to the door. "So?"

"So?"

"So, *you*."

"I'm in the CIA. I was sent here to infiltrate a gang of international terrorists."

I thought that was cute. She did not.

"I'm on my way to Los Angeles but this is as far as I got when my car broke down."

"What's in Los Angeles?"

"I'm going to be a director."

"A movie director?"

"Yeah."

"That's cool. How do you do that? I mean, how do you get that job?"

I hadn't thought that far ahead. I'd driven hundreds of miles and at no point did I think 'How am I going to do this?' That's the problem with dreamers, right? They're always already there in their mind.

I told her that I only lied about my mom getting a job here because the truth had landed me zero jobs. No one wants to hire someone who's just going to leave.

She put her hand on my guitar case and asked me to play for her.

"There's no guitar in there, I just use it as a suitcase."

"Did you ever have a guitar?"

"No."

She was ready to ask, "then why the case?" but didn't. She opened it without asking permission. "Alice in Chains. Nirvana. The Doors, a whole lot of Doors. Nine Inch Nails. Radiohead. A shit ton. Korn. Shit, you're a 90s poster boy, aren't you?"

"And you're a goth poser girl, aren't you?"

Before she gave me the look, I knew I shouldn't have said it. There was no apologizing—we were too new—she would have to either let the seconds elapse or storm out. "What kind of name is 'Sanford' anyways? Your parents like junkyards so much they named you after 'Sanford & Son'?"

"I'm named after my grandpa."

"Is your dad 'Sanford' too? That would make you 'Sanford the third'."

"We don't have thirds, or juniors."

"What?"

"Nothing."

"What's this?" she asked as she pulled a book from the case. "Sim Seder?" At that moment I realized I had put everything Jewish in the guitar case. Separated out, these objects would be of little consequence. Together, they made me a Super Jew. I told her it was a prayer book, explained that Hebrew is read from right to left when she told me the book was backwards. That I was Jewish.

"No shit! I've never met a Jew before!"

Her excitement was both a relief and loud. I wondered what a passerby would have thought hearing that. Was she a hooker excited for a kosher, circumcised cock?

"That's so cool!"

"Is it?"

"Dude, I got nothing against Jesus but fuck, man, that's all people talk about here."

"Is that why you dress like that? The makeup?"

She scowled at me and told me she dressed like she did because she wanted to dress like that.

"At least I think I'm Jewish, my dad is but my mom's kind of not."

"What do you mean?"

"She converted."

"Shut up. You're Jewish, and I *know* you."

She put my yarmulke on her head and smiled. Took out a photograph from my Bar Mitzvah and laughed at the dorky 13-year-old boy with thick glasses pretending to read the Torah. I felt the flushed heat in my cheeks and found my cigarettes on the dresser. Now holding the upper hand, she took off her coat and set it down on the bed.

"I can't read your handwriting."

"What?"

"This. I can't read it, is it Hebrew?"

I took the stack of papers and told her no, it was English, I just had bad handwriting.

"Can *you* read it?"

"Of course, I can."

She took my cigarette then arranged the pillows and laid down on the bed. I told her it was a sad story and I didn't want to depress her. She pointed to her black clothing and purple lips as evidence that I was incapable of depressing her.

"What's it about?"

"It's about what happened, you know, to my family. During the war, the Holocaust."

This was going the exact opposite of how I wanted it to go. The plan, *my* plan, was that she would show up to my motel room after her shift. Last night. Specifically, at night. Preferably with alcohol. I would have told her that I'm going to be a famous film director and that would make her want me and, in the morning, we'd get pancakes.

"Read it to me."

"The whole thing?"

"Yes."

I didn't want to. These were things I *had* to keep; heirlooms meant for a bottom dresser drawer in a Los Angeles mansion. I got a replacement cigarette, lit it, and by the time I sat down on the opposite bed she was wearing my gold chain with the Star of David. She had gone full Goth Jew, and I was both aroused and confused.

"Sit here," she said as she patted the bed she occupied. I obliged and took a deep drag; I hadn't read this since I wrote it. I warned her that chronology was not my grandmother's strong suit and her accent made some of it a little incoherent. She didn't care.

"When he went back after the first trip, ship was full. Grandfather was ready to commit suicide. Stayed with Uncle Sam in New York after getting off the ship. Went back because things were bad in New York. Went to Romania.

They lost everything—Grandfather returned.

Sanford..."

"That's you!" Mandy interjected. I looked over at her. "Sorry, continue."

"Sanford, born in Solotvena—Austria Hungary. 1913. Father—lost everything— drinking—returned to U.S. because no money.

Sanford—5th grade. Good student. Good memory. Left for Bucharest at age 15 (?) after father left for New York. Grandmother did not know how to write.

To Bucharest, 1930, after grandfather came to U.S. Worked as a carpenter—he had trained for this in Toshnet.

Sanford. Bucharest to Budapest. 1939. War on. Became better there (Budapest). Rumors that Germans occupied Budapest. 1941. Hungarians took him to working.

Bucharest—made furniture for a company.

Met Helena in Solotvena—knew her sister who was friends with his cousin. 1941. Helena and Sanford were in a theater. Sanford said he heard a rumor that the Germans had occupied Budapest. When they left the theater there were Germans controlling the streets. They took the theater as barracks.

1940—Helena goes to Budapest. Sanford called and asked her to a soccer game. Jews now had to report to the German authority. They took the men away to work for them. They took him (Sanford) to the Russian front. He ran to the Russian side.

Czechoslovakia went to fight against Germany. There were a number of Czechs in Russia as part of the Russian Army to have a Czech Republic. Russians hated the

Jews more than the Germans. How many Jews?"

"Huh?"

"What?" I asked her.

"What does that mean? 'How many Jews?'"

I told her sometimes it was hard to understand what she said with her accent.

"Who's Helena?"

"My grandmother."

"He injured his right elbow and was unable to straighten his arm. This happened soon after he started fighting. I have a Russian document indicating the wound was from a shell, a plastic elbow was used to repair the wound in 1953.

Returned to Budapest in 1945. Helena did not hear from Sanford from the time he left until the time he came back. He wrote to his parents to ask if they knew what had happened to Helena. Sanford's parents had thought that he had died, and this letter was the first word that he had survived the war. He found Helena, they married in 1946. Received a pension and a store selling gifts and cigarettes. 3,000

crowns working for the government, but he made more than this as there was a large black market in American cigarettes.

Helena's father had a store, leather to make shoes. She worked in a textile store. Went to Budapest. Brother-in-law was held up. Arrested because he was a Jew and was in jail without clothes. Helena brought him clothes and was to only stay the weekend. She found a job making sweaters and stayed.

Solotvena, population less than 1,000. Hungarian Romanian, less than half of whom were Jewish. Solotvena was old-fashioned, women had to shave their hair when they married.

Walked into a factory and told she had a job. She would not have to work on Saturdays but would make less money. She was sent to a factory across the street with an Orthodox owner who told his partner he had to give her a job. She did not know how to sew or knit, perhaps the job was offered because she was young and attractive. She worked there for four

years knitting five days per week and made good money.

Germans took over. Helena had to go to a large school to work for the Germans. She dug trenches for two weeks and did not have enough to eat. Hundreds of people were sleeping there. Hungarian SS was called Nielosh, The Arrow Cross Party.

Most Jews that were not in school were taken away by the Hungarian SS and sent to 'work camps'—Auschwitz.

They put stars on Jewish homes. Helena got into school because someone from her hometown knew a general or had connections. She was friendly with the sister.

"What sister?" Mandy asked.

I reread the sentence twice. "I'm not sure," I told her, and kept reading.

If you were Jewish and not in school— you were gone.

After digging trenches for several weeks, the Romanian soldiers came and they had a chance to leave the school and not be watched. The feeling was that they would

be sent to camps. Helena hesitated to leave the school—she was concerned her landlady would not take her back. The school leaders insisted. She left, as they feared for their lives.

Raul Wallenberg helped the people at the school. It was because of him that the people in the school were not deported.

Of Helena's family, one brother survived. He was killed in a traffic accident in Israel. Per letter from the Israeli Consulate General Office: Accident, May 5, 1949. Burial, June 6, 1949. Her mother died at age 53 of elevated blood pressure and diabetes. Her father, age 63, died in a concentration camp. Three sisters died in camps, and another died at home from a brain tumor. One brother froze to death after being taken away.

Back at her apartment, she was sheltered by her landlady. She wanted to pay the custodian but he would not accept money. The custodian said, "I'm so glad you are back."

The Germans were fighting the Russians or a Romanian contingent of the

Russian forces. Shortly after, Budapest was liberated by the Russians—1945.

Russians now occupy Budapest. Could not get food. Left for Bucharest by train. Had to be careful, Russian soldiers were raping young women.

Helena was at the Bucharest Joint Distribution Committee for three months. She stayed with a nice family and the landlady stood in line for bread. They were able to eat and had money for the room through the Joint Distribution Committee. No work, though. She wrote to her former boss to ask if there was work. He told her to return.

There were two young girls on the train from Solotvena. On the way to Bucharest, they got off the train for a sleepover in a small town. They went to the mayor and acquired lodging. Helena went out to see someone she knew and when she returned the young girls were crying. Soldiers had come and said they would be coming back for them later that night. Helena told them they had to hide. They climbed fences and went as far as they could from town. When they awoke, they found that they had slept in a cemetery.

They went back to the train station where the mayor's wife told them that the Russians did come back and took away her 12-year-old daughter.

Now in Budapest, she had the same job as before and lived in the same apartment. After a short time, Sanford returned. They married on January 13, 1946, and then moved to Franitiscovy Lazne where his store was located. The town had health baths.

Helena visited Cleveland, Ohio, and Sanford stayed in Europe. One day Helena came home crying. She did not like America and could not wait to get home. The main meal was dinner, not lunch. Here, she worked seven days, 12 hours per day. In Europe the stores closed at lunch and on weekends. She had a nicer life.

When Helena returned to Franitiscovy Lazne, the communists had taken over. Sanford had contacted her in Cleveland and told her the situation and that he did *not want her to return. However, her visa did not allow her to stay.*

It was not safe to talk. They stood and watched how you voted and told people where to put the ballot. This did not affect material wealth, but freedoms such as speech and voting. They felt that they could not stay.

Sanford had a visa from 1941. Molly had done the paperwork for Sanford to come but he was already in the army. The visa was still good. Eight months later they came to Cleveland."

I put the papers down and looked at Mandy. She told me that most people here didn't believe the Holocaust even happened. That it was just to make people feel bad for the Jews. She asked me what had happened to Sanford, I told her he died before I was born. And Helena? She had cancer.

"It would have been better if you had videotaped this instead of writing it down," Mandy said, me wanting to be a director and all. I think she was right, once

I made it in Hollywood I'd go back and do
it right. All professional and what not.

January 10

Fridays still feel weird to me without Shabbos candles. I think my mother lit them out of obligation, not a sense of religion or belief. Regardless, a habit is just that. My new Friday routine is making milkshakes for high school kids and pretending not to notice them pouring liquor into the thick glasses. To take their shit even though their pockets are only slightly lusher than mine. It doesn't take long for a waiter to daydream about quitting his job in an extravagant and very public way. That release is longed for from the first day they remove the 'trainee' badge and set you free in a section. It's spoken about openly.

I've heard Carla and Patty both describe their exits. The former, she will stand on the lunch counter and give bellowing 'fuck yous' to every customer, then to Terry, and finally, Frank—all while her two middle fingers are prominently displayed. Patty, well, she wanted to break some shit when she left and cut off Terry's balls.

It's time for my shift.

♦ ♦ ♦

I waited on the old men in the smoking section. Oh fuck, did they hate that. Patty wanted Mandy to do it. "Your table's here, freak," she said. Yet it's been two days since I told Mandy the truth and I still have a job, so it was a gesture I felt necessary. A nickel. Each of them gave me a single nickel as a tip—all because I don't have tits.

"I'm going to give that Doug guy regular instead of decaf next time, he's the worst," I complained to Mandy. She took me over to the coffee station and pulled down an urn with the orange band and showed it to me. "Yeah," I said, "orange is decaf."

"Not this one," and she pointed to a little hand-drawn 'x' in black marker on the handle. "Well, it's still decaf," she leaned in to whisper, "and piss." She saw the look on my face, an awestruck and impressed combination. "Ever since he pulled at my shirt to look at my breasts and spanked my ass, he's been drinking my piss."

"No," I said in disbelief.

"He makes us brew a new pot for him, and I take great joy in cheerfully reassuring him that his coffee is decaf before I pour it. He got lucky tonight."

I asked her if she did anything to Carla and Patty for calling her 'freak,' but she said no, she can tell the difference between juvenile insecurity and just plain meanness.

I told her that she's too intelligent to be working as a waitress. Also, in regard to

Doug, that I didn't have many heroes in this world, but she was one of them. She leaned in to kiss me and I moved my head back. Once she didn't meet my expected lips, she opened her eyes and immediately the embarrassment hit.

"Wait," I pleaded, but she had turned and went behind the kitchen. "Wait!" She opened the walk-in for an escape but didn't check the dishwasher magnet. She, and I, saw Terry's pale, hairy ass bucking against a bent-over Patty.

"You fucking whore!" Mandy yelled, then slammed the door. I stood. Stunned, both by the situation between Mandy and I and the visual assault I had just been dealt. By the time I had my bearings, Mandy had slipped outside through the emergency door. It, like most things in here, was broken, no alarms and no surprises.

I saw her walking fast past the dumpsters and then she ran. I slipped, again. "How many fucking times am I going to slip on this God damn ice!" I screamed as my back throbbed.

"Mandy!" I yelled as she opened her car door. She got in and slammed the door. My broken self made it to the window and she stared at the steering wheel.

"I'm so fucking stupid!" she belted as she pounded on the steering wheel.

"No, you're not!"

"Yeah, well how could I totally misread that? I misread everything!"

"That's not true."

"You've known me for like, a week!"

I knelt down to be at eye level. "I like you," my voice elevated to compensate for the closed window. She didn't look at me. "I really do, a lot."

"You're just making me more confused."

"Can I tell you another Jewish story?" She didn't say no. "When I was in Hebrew School, we did this play. I don't remember what it was about. Shit, I don't even think there was an audience. But I remember the teacher put makeup on us. The boys and the girls. This rouge shit that made all our cheeks bright red and she put lipstick on our lips. A lot of lipstick. I have no idea what that play was about, but I do remember the taste of all that lipstick on my lips. I hated it, and all I could think about was getting it off of me. It's not that I don't like you, it's that I can't kiss you with lipstick on. Any girl. I just can't do it, so, I'm sorry." She didn't move. "I didn't mean to embarrass you."

The door handle clicked, and she slowly climbed out of the car. We stood staring at each other, she wanted to know my sincerity and when she was satisfied, she wiped a frozen tear from her cheek. We walked back to the restaurant and I opened the front door for her. Frank was standing in the office doorway and watched us come in from the cold.

"Hi Frank," she said to him quietly. He mustered a miniscule smile then returned to the office. A four-top walked in and I sat them in the main dining area then told Patty she had a table. I went to the back and Terry asked me politely for one of my 'good' cigarettes. I obliged and had one with him.

♦ ♦ ♦

I hate this hotel room. I've layered my feet in socks and they're still cold. What I wouldn't do for a drink. I wonder if she only tried to kiss me to say she did it, to say she kissed a Jew. I still don't have any dishes. Everything I eat in this room is pre-packaged, pre-contained and preserved. Some nights, when I can't sleep, I gorge on Hostess fruit pies and milk to make my stomach heavy.

January 11

"Do you think I look ugly?" Her hair was without the scrunchie and followed the hills of her powder blue puffy hood. I couldn't tell in the dim yellow light if she was wearing makeup, but I was sure there was no lipstick on her lips. I leaned in, kissed her, and let my lips linger. I told her that she didn't have to change anything for me.

"I wanted to. I've wanted to for a while." She told me she had outgrown that phase and only kept it going to annoy her mom.

She asked me if I drink and pulled a fifth of rum from her bag.

She brought cans of Coke and we spilled out half of each in the sink and filled the cans back up with rum. I had made the difficult decision to not bring my stereo, so we listened to MTV on the television. I intended to buy a new one in Los Angeles. A nice one.

I tried to reach under her shirt while we made out but she stopped me. She just wanted to kiss. She asked me how long until my car is fixed. A week, maybe two, I told her.

"Can I go with you?" she asked me. I told her yes, but that my grandmother would not be too happy that I was dating a gentile.

"What's a gentile?"

"Someone who isn't Jewish."

"Then we just don't tell her."

I didn't think she was serious, it was easy to spout grandiose plans drunk on rum in the arms of a new lover. The decision becomes serious in the morning light. When the decision was closer. Real.

I'd mastered the art of how to disappear completely, but I'd found it was not for everyone. And when you surface from the ocean depths it was up to you to pretend that you were never truly gone.

January 12

Working Sundays was a requirement, although the restaurant was closed on Monday for the staff to recuperate from the ungodly Godliness that descends once church has ended. Frank, for all his nothingness, understands the staff's limits. It seems that a good time to sin was immediately following forgiveness. Gluttony, I see you. Lust? Lust lives in a walk-in cooler in the back of a dirty restaurant along the interstate.

"So," Patty said while I put in an order, "you're a Jew?"

I told her I was.

"That's cool. Don't tell Carla."

I told her I wasn't planning on it.

"They're shitty tippers, these 'churchies,' but there are a lot of them, so we make out all right."

"One time I got a Jesus pamphlet instead of a tip."

"Some people suck."

I guess now I'm 'the Jew.' Maybe I can't trust Mandy. One week, maybe two, and I'll be able to fix my car. To get out of this place and continue west. How can I go after something as big as this with someone who I can't trust? No, she can't go with me. I wish I could leave now. I wonder who else she told.

"Are you ready for this?" Terry asked me. I told him I guessed so. I prepared double the coffee and grinned as I thought about what the 'x' on the one urn meant as the coffee dripped.

Sunday's forced Frank to actually do something, and he stood at the host stand practicing his smile. I could see his stained tank top under his see-through dress shirt. His blue tie with pink flowers.

They piled in, stuck close together from the front door to the first row of booths. Frank and Patty alternated seating each family. Each elderly couple. The men who arrived alone went for the lunch counter and were all gruff with beards that hid their faces. Mandy, per Carla's orders, was responsible for the counter. This meant she wouldn't get as many tables. It also meant she was the dishwasher. She was pissed, but I was still upset that she had exposed what I assumed was a secret.

I expected suits and ties, that's how it was at synagogue. Or the fancy hats I'd seen Black Christian women wear on television shows. There was none of that. Mostly collared flannel shirts tucked into blue jeans. Oversized belt buckles. Maybe that was a necktie to them. The children ate ravenously and climbed from the top of the booths to the floor and then back again. The fathers and mothers of families who sat along the windows smoked deeply.

Teenage girls whispered between tables. Teenage boys stared awkwardly.

I expected to overhear some talk of church. Of Jesus. A preacher's sermon dissected. Maybe they were waiting until they'd had time to reflect. Maybe those conversations happen on Sunday evenings.

Frank was at the register, sweating as the line built. Each server sucked down a cigarette in the back when we could. Terry smoked while he cooked and leaned down so he would be hidden from the non-smoking tables in his line of sight. They wouldn't understand like those near the windows would.

We all met at the back table when the rush ended to smoke. I gave Terry one of mine. Mandy suggested a united front to pressure Frank into hiring a new dishwasher. She received muted enthusiasm; the others are never stuck dish washing on Sundays.

◆ ◆ ◆

Mandy drove me back to my motel room after work.

"Why did you tell Patty I'm Jewish?"

"I don't know, I just think it's cool."

I told her okay but not to tell anyone else. She told me I should come over for dinner tomorrow night. The restaurant will be closed and we need to save all our money for going to Los Angeles. I couldn't tell her I was having second thoughts about her going. I never thought she was serious to begin with. Maybe I'd just leave without her. I'd just go and be gone and after a while it would be as if I was never here.

January 13

Mandy lived in a trailer park. The smell of cat urine and stale litter hit you. I guessed that was why she wore the perfume. There were benches on each side of the kitchen table. Everything was close. Claustrophobic. A cat rubbed against my leg.

Her mother used a spatula to cut into a lasagna and, after serving us, sat down. There was toasted white bread with butter and garlic powder on a plate in the center of the table. Mandy poured an orange drink from a plastic pitcher into four glasses. We all held hands as she said a prayer to Jesus. Then silence as we ate for several minutes. Years.

"I'm glad you're not wearing all that makeup," her mother said, "made you look all dark. Depressing."

Her father told me that Mandy wouldn't tell them too much about me, just that she met a boy. "Not out of the ordinary, I guess, for a girl to be embarrassed by her father." He winked at her. As if to prove his point she blushed.

Mandy told them that my mom moved here.

"I was on my way to Los Angeles," I said with a mouthful of lasagna, "my car broke down." I didn't need to lie to them. "Got the job at the restaurant so I could pay to get it repaired." He asked me what was wrong with it. "Transmission went out. Clutch is going too."

"How long you think till you've got the money saved?" I told him a week or two. He told me I must have saved a lot already, considering the cost of the repairs. "Not to be prying, or inconsiderate," he added,

"I'm just saying I know how much Mandy brings home, and you got the same job."

I felt my appetite leave me at once. Had I miscalculated? How *badly* had I miscalculated? Even with depriving myself meals most days except at the restaurant, had my modest accommodations been dragging down any chance of leaving this place? I was a transient here, with no plans to put down roots—nor had I acted in a way to facilitate acceptance. Mandy had sought me out, I did not pursue her. The thought of a life here of orange drink and cat piss. The thought that I would have to call home and admit defeat.

"Mandy," her mother said, "do you think your friend would like to come to church with us next Sunday?"

"I have to work Sundays, mom, you know that."

"Well maybe just him, then?" I had instantly become invisible; I had no other way to explain it other than it was fucking awkward.

"He works with me, that's how we met."

I wanted to reach out and touch both their shoulders and reassure them, 'Ladies, I'm right here, everything is okay.' Instead, I told her I've never been to church.

"I'm Jewish."

What did I care what they thought? I could choose not to see them again, not so with my coworkers—at least not for a week. A month? Two? And in that moment, I waited for any reaction while they waited for a continuation.

"Well, shit!" her dad finally responded, "and here we started off dinner with a prayer to Jesus."

"I am so sorry for that," her mother added.

"Do you keep kosher?" her father asked.

"Not really, mostly when I'm home."

It was by habit that I called where I had left, home.

"I don't think this dinner was kosher," she fretted.

"It was wonderful," I said, "that's what it was, really wonderful. Thank you."

She smiled that relieving smile one does when the offense perceived has not been taken as such.

♦ ♦ ♦

"God damn cat piss," he said as he handed me a beer in the driveway. "Mandy wanted a cat, so we got a cat. I told her she has to take care of it and you know what she does? She lets it run all over the trailer park so of course it gets pregnant. Now I got five cats and two women who won't let me get rid of even one of 'em." He had taken on a more colloquial pattern of speech. Blasphemy, curse words, and dropped letters were now in play. "Fuck I can't stand going to church," he stated, as if confessing for the first time, "best place to find a liar is on a church pew. How often you go to Temple?" I told him I've been once or twice since my Bar Mitzvah. "You got liars there?"

"Probably, but mostly I just felt kinda judged."

"Yeah, I get that."

"I guess I felt bad for my parents having to hear all those other parents telling them where their kids are going to college. Didn't want them to get judged for me, you know?"

He told me everyone has an idea of what it means to be successful. To have 'made it.' No matter where you go, what their religion.

"I guess I feel it more, so much talk about it."

"Are your folks embarrassed by you? By what you have, or haven't become?"

I told him they've never said so.

"Maybe you just assumed they were embarrassed without really knowing. Maybe they think their kid's got it all figured out and these other kids are just doing what they're supposed to do." He put up his forefinger and counted, "School, work, family, death. That's what they've got coming to them. Nothing more, maybe less."

"Is that what you got?"

He took a shovel, scraped the snow off two wooden steps and we sat down. "Do you know what life is, Sanford?" I told him I did not. "Life is suffering. At least, according to the Buddha. Desire, he says, is the cause of this suffering. If you want to understand yourself, get yourself some Buddhism. Some Lao Tzu. Go East, young man. If you want to be accepted by those in a church or a synagogue or a mosque, you'll have to pretend to care about the judgmental, hypocritical sinners by pretending you're someone you're not." He put his arm on my shoulder, "You will always desire to be you, and for that desire you will suffer."

"But you go to church?"

"Yeah, well, society here says I gotta go, but I don't have to *be* there," and he put his finger against his head. I lit a cigarette and told him how much I was quoted for repairing my car. He said they underquoted me by a lot so they'd jack it up once they had my car and I had no choice but to pay. The mechanic's where he drives truck told him that. Those that break down on the interstate get jacked up real good coming through here, they figure they'll never come back. They never do. Just a mile marker to something better.

♦ ♦ ♦

Mandy drove me back to the motel. I told her about her dad and Buddhism; she said Vietnam made him that way. I kissed her in the car and touched her breast over her shirt, I didn't want to push it.

I want to be warm. Somewhere where the seasons don't touch the months.

January 14

I called three shops this morning, two quoted me double what the tow truck driver had when I first arrived. One, triple. I called Amtrak and I can take four big bags with me. That would mean I'd need a ride to the train station—Mandy, and she thinks she's coming with me. She isn't serious, is she? If she was, she'd have suggested taking her car days ago. Would it make it? Would I feel guilt for having her run away with me? Her parents seemed so nice. Maybe they would be okay with it.

Fuck my shit car. Fuck this shit place and fuck this cold. In a nutshell.

No work today. No Mandy today. Just me.

♦ ♦ ♦

If someone is standing at your doorway holding tacos, you invite them inside. You just do. Danger be damned. She brought a portable stereo. We ate the tacos. We shared sips of whiskey straight and chased it with a 2-liter of Sprite and listened to The Doors. Her kisses forced me to the bed closest the window and she took off her shirt and bra as she straddled me. There was this synchronicity which I had never felt with a girl. Every move we made was understood and propelled us forward. Every touch was perfect, every new position fluid and when we had climaxed, we fell into each other's arms. I was finally warm. I felt, if only for these moments, a sense of home in a transient place. That elusive comfort which hides itself so well in uncertainty.

January 15

Heavy snow. A dinner shift that ran into late night old man coffee. Mandy was working a double and couldn't give me a ride. I kept thinking seven days more, if only to soothe my sanity.

I sat down at the back table to have a smoke before my shift. Carla was there, I said hello and she ignored me. Put out her recently lit cigarette and walked away. Mandy told me that Carla put me in smoking tonight, then snuck me a kiss. Something felt off, but the walk-in was set to 'dirty,' so at least that seemed right.

No one came in for dinner. No one. Blizzard conditions. Frank hid in his office. We smoked in the back. Terry made his own recipes and had us taste-test. Considering the limited ingredients available, everything tasted like a rip-off of a menu item. We humored him.

"This is so good, Terry!"

"Seriously, you should be a chef somewhere."

I wonder if he imagined himself in some fancy restaurant in New York City. Paris. Perhaps he didn't, perhaps he had given up on hope, but didn't quite have the cutting edge of anger that accompanies utter despair.

Frank appeared but did not come too close. He just stood there, his hands at his sides, then walked away. Everyone knew what he meant, except me. There was a table to be sat. The four old men and their fearless leader, Doug. They were like the post office, neither rain nor sleet nor

fucking blizzard could keep them from their ceramic cups. Eggshell white for regular. Brown for decaf.

"Shit," Mandy whispered, "I just peed." I heard them tell Carla that they didn't want me and then they stared at me as they walked by so there was no confusion. The feeling was mutual, I didn't want their nickels.

"Hi, Doug!" I yelled as I stood behind the lunch counter. I waved my arm to emphasize my greeting. He was not amused.

"Yeah," Terry said through laughter behind the kitchen window, "fuck that guy."

I grabbed a Styrofoam cup from a rack and walked swiftly to the employee bathroom. Spun my apron around and let loose into the cup. Mandy was at the coffee station and I slid the cup to her, hiding it with my body from the rest of the staff. "For Doug's coffee."

She poured it into the glass pot and I gagged. She threw the cup into the waste bin, put her lips next to my ear, and said slowly in a sultry voice, "Teamwork," she paused, "makes the dream work." We had become the Bonnie and Clyde of pissing in an old man's coffee.

"I thought I was in smoking?" I asked Carla, knowing the answer, when she took the pots.

"They don't want you," she said with a clip of anger and walked away. I watched her bend over as she poured, giving each old man a good show, her gold cross dangling between her breasts. She looked up and her stare closed the distance between smoking and the lunch counter.

Two men sat down at the lunch counter, took off their bright orange caps and lit cigarettes. Mandy poured them black coffee and filled their thermoses. They didn't speak, and once their cigarettes were extinguished, they lumbered back to pickup trucks with snowplows and amber lights that illuminated Terry every five seconds. His face was framed in the kitchen window and I could sense he wanted to be one of them. To have a coffee and a smoke when he wanted. To see

accomplishment in every pass. There was no undercooked, no overcooked. There was no gray area, either the lot was plowed—or it wasn't. No one to give him shit simply because they didn't like the way he looked. How he carried himself. Spoke.

The old men watched the plows reverse, and in the snowy white air, their rear red lights disappeared quickly. Doug muttered disdain as another pickup pulled in and shone its lights in their eyes. No plow.

"Sup, old man?" a teenage boy taunted Doug as he stared. The three boys sat down at the corner booth in smoking.

"They're mine," Carla snipped. She kissed one of the boys and he pinched her ass. I flipped the rubbery cucumbers in the salad bar. Picked up a metal ladle and watched the bleu cheese chunks plop into the white dressing. "They want you," she told me, then walked into the back.

The boy she kissed was wearing a mechanics shirt. It said 'Kyle' in cursive. I thought that I could befriend him and he would fix my car. Reasoned that perhaps he bought the shirt at a thrift store and was not a mechanic. "What can I get you to drink?" They all wanted Cokes. Light ice. Kyle told me to hurry the fuck up.

"Too much ice," he said as I sat down the glass. I asked him how many cubes they wanted. He told me four. I went back to the ice bin and counted them out.

Kyle took a sip. "Not cold enough." I stood there not knowing what to do. He used the back of his hand to push the glass off the table. It shattered at my feet.

"Oops," his friend said.

"Looks like you've got some cleaning to do," Kyle added. I felt the urge to punch him in his face. I imagined the blood spurting from his nose as adrenaline made me superhuman and his friends could not pull me off. I thought of pissing in their drinks. Of having a baseball bat and swinging through their skulls. I heard Carla refilling the old man's coffee behind me and I looked at her. She smiled.

I swept the glass shards and dirty liquid into the dustpan. Mopped the floor, set up a caution sign, and with my pen in hand, I started over. "What can I get you?"

"You can get the fuck out of here," a friend said. I just stared. "We don't want no Jew here," Kyle clarified.

"It's Strawberry Fest," I said, "we have strawberry pie, strawberry shakes, and strawberry shortcake. Ice cream on your pie is a dollar extra."

"Did you hear me?" Kyle stood up. I told him I did.

"Chicken fried steak is on special." I could feel my heartbeat throb my neck. I hadn't been in a fight since middle school. Each in Jay's backyard. Each premeditated and at the fence gate we'd hand over anything we wished wouldn't be broken in the scuffle. Watches. A gold necklace with a Star of David. Another with Vishnu. Friends would encircle the combatants and act as judges to determine the winner of each petty grievance. The worst we could expect was a bloody nose. This was different. I didn't know his intent; I didn't know his capabilities. I looked around for my co-workers, but there were only the old men who shied away when I made eye contact.

I smelled the cigarettes on his breath and asked him if we wanted the chicken fried steak. "No, I ain't interested in chicken, fried, steak."

"Fuck you," I whispered. He asked me what I said. "You heard me."

"Say it again."

I swallowed. Hard. "Fuck you," clearly, and with volume. As his hands gripped my throat, I thought maybe they had never met a Jew. To have gone their whole lives without having seen the ones they hate, the opportunity could not be missed. He flung me around, pushed me into the emergency door and the screeching alarm sounded, of course this one worked. Then onto their table which brought another glass crashing to the floor. His friend poured the remaining coke onto my face. Then ketchup. Then mustard. The door closed and the alarm stopped. I fought off one of Kyle's hands and he brought his forehead down on my nose. I felt the back of my head hit the table and his forehead smeared with the ketchup and mustard. Maybe my blood. I brought a butter knife to his neck and his friend snatched it and put it to mine.

"This is what we do," Kyle exclaimed between breaths, "to Jews that come here." He looked up to his left and stopped. His hands loosened enough for me to look as well. We had an audience now. Terry, whom I had never seen leave the kitchen or back area, was standing there, in the smoking section that ran along the front of the restaurant with its large windows. Carla, Mandy, and Patty were behind him.

It was Frank, though, that had given him pause. Sweaty, weird Frank who had no emotions, but now had a revolver pointed at Kyle's head. He didn't say anything; Kyle simply knew to release his grip. I guess the only time someone actually needs to say something while holding a gun is in the movies, I thought, but how would I know? I'd never even seen a gun before this moment except at the hip of a cop. I wanted him to say something. Anything. For anything was dramatic when a hand was on the trigger. I would remember that when I got to Hollywood.

Kyle's friends slid slowly from the booth and all three boys walked towards Frank. He put his free hand up. They stopped. He pointed behind them to the emergency door. The alarm blared again and they went out into the blizzard holding their coats.

Frank lowered the gun, surveyed the smoking section, then went into his office and closed the door. I lit a cigarette and sat down at a clean table. Mandy went and got a wet dish towel. I cleaned my face. I could taste blood. "Frank says you're cut," Patty said, "so you can go home early." Mandy told me she'd take me home if I stayed until her shift was over, but I wanted to be anywhere but there. She said she was sorry, there wasn't much more she could have said. I'm sure that once I left, the old men had something new to discuss.

◆ ◆ ◆

The wind hit sideways. Hard. My face was wet from the snow when I entered the convenience store. Went straight for the cooler and took a six-pack of Budweiser. Down the aisle a pint of Jack. I set the alcohol on the counter and asked for a pack of Reds. He stared at me, the blush of my cheeks from the cold that made me look even younger. The dried blood underneath my nose. The snow melting from my cap.

I stared back. His wheezing breaths. The hairy gut I could see where his t-shirt didn't quite make it. His bushy eyebrows and aggressive nose hairs. His right hand went to the register to press the buttons and his left packed my items into a brown paper bag. I handed him a twenty-dollar bill and he returned the change.

"Some days," he said as I pushed open the door, "are just shitty days." I nodded in agreement, walked to my room and stripped off my clothes. Waited the few minutes for the brown water to pass and stepped into the hot shower. Watched the blood that the warmth had rekindled circle down the drain. Felt the bruise on the back of my head. Punched the tile and cursed out loud the predicament I found myself in. The six dollars added to my paycheck for a night's work. All I was doing here was going broke and soon I'd have to take the last of my dollars to the bus station and return home a failure. The one child who didn't understand the importance of education, who sat up late in his room writing poetry in an incense fog while the others rested for exams. That dreamer, that oddity, who didn't take it seriously and was now standing on his parent's doorstep, hat in hand.

I tried to shudder the thoughts of failure, to jolt my mind to think of anything else. I let the shampoo sting my eyes and dug my fingernails into the soap to spend several minutes removing the soft white uncomfortable feeling. Took swigs of Jack and kept reaching for the lit cigarette in the sink.

Dried myself and put on a shirt that had me wondering where the nearest laundromat was. My work clothes smelled of grease and cigarettes and cleanser. I searched my memory for any stories from Hebrew School, any parables, nothing. The Torah. The Talmud. Anything to give me strength in this motel bathroom. I couldn't remember anything. What good was religion if it didn't help you in situations such as these? What good was having a religion if you'd never felt anything in your heart? I punched myself in the jaw. "Stupid!" Again. Harder. "Stupid!" I found the beers and opened one.

A knock on the door. They had found me, and they were here to finish the job. To kill the heretic Jew. I put my eye to the lowest corner of the window to spy a figure. It was Mandy, I let her in. She brought McDonald's.

January 16

Philosophy dulls the hangover to a whispered sensation, and I was feeling quite philosophical the morning after. Those thoughts were aided by strong motel bathroom coffee and cigarettes.

"Your grandma saved those two girls," Mandy said while reading the oral history. "Helena went out to see someone she knew," she continued when I didn't respond, "and when she returned the young girls were crying. Soldiers had come and said they would be coming back for them later that night. Helena told them they had to hide."

That whisper was *still* a sensation, and I didn't engage. "She saved lives, that's not something a lot of people can say." She told me I should be proud. I told her I guessed so. "They climbed fences and went as far as they could from town. They went back to the train station where the mayor's wife told them that the Russians did come back and took away her 12-year-old daughter."

"She died," I said.

"Who?"

"The mayor's daughter."

"How do you know that?"

"That's how it was. She was killed or she was raped and then killed."

"You can't be sure of that."

"I can."

"How?"

"You've never looked in the eyes of anyone who was there."

"No, I haven't."

"Well if you do, you'll be sure of it too."

She asked me if I think Frank saved my life. I told her I was scared but I think if they would've wanted to kill me, they would have brought a baseball bat or a knife or a gun. Probably would have waited until I was alone.

"I guess Kyle just wanted to look like a badass in front of his friends."

"So he *was* wearing his name on his shirt?"

"Yeah, that's Carla's boyfriend."

She put the paper back in the guitar case and sat down on the floor next to me, our backs against the dresser. I told her I'm leaving, that I couldn't go back to the restaurant. Taking what I could on the train and leaving. Tomorrow, maybe the day after. She said I didn't need to take a train, that she was going with me.

"I need to do this on my own," I told her.

"No one does anything on their own."

"They do, and I will."

"Have you maybe thought that I want to leave too? Not just be a tagalong on your epic journey?" I didn't answer. "You think I want to spend the rest of my life here? As some gas station restaurant waitress? I want to do things too, Sanford."

"Like what?"

"It doesn't matter! But if I stay here this is all I'll be."

"Go to college."

"With what fucking money? You saw where I live. I guess I'm just some girl to you, to make you feel less alone. I thought, just maybe, this was *my* opportunity to get out, that you would see that." I lit a cigarette and avoided her eyes. "No, you're too much of a selfish prick to get that."

She threw on her coat and stood with the door open, allowing me to respond, to defend her characterization. The door slammed and I listened to her car drive off over the salt, snow and slush.

January 17

I rehearsed my words in the cold brightness as I walked. *I'm sorry.* The crunch of snow tamped down by plow truck wheels driven by men in orange wool caps. *I was being selfish.* Black ice treachery on the overpass. *Come with me. I want—you to come with me.* Gasoline pumps and rainbow pools where the liquid had dripped, melting the snow. *Sometimes I can be selfish.* Carla in the smoking section through the large windows, bussing a table. *You're not just some girl.*

I love you, no, I care about you. Frank at the office door, I nodded, and he nodded back. *Maybe 'I love you,' from some dramatic movie.* I poured myself a cup of coffee and took a handful of creams and sugars to the back table. Looked at the dishwasher magnet and listened to the muted moans from the walk-in. Carla paused when she saw me, then walked past. She grabbed her coat and hat and left through the broken emergency door.

I laid a Red on the table at an empty chair in preparation for Terry's shortness of breath and need of one. *I'm sorry.* I was. The moans stopped. *I was being selfish.*

Terry lit the cigarette I left for him and nodded to thank me. It was another minute before Patty exited the walk-in.

"The freak called in," she told me. I guessed I had more time to rehearse.

"Carla just left."

"Fuck."

"Friday night high school fuckheads, all for me and you." The cigarette smoke did not hide the smell of sex and sweat.

Patty banged on the wall shared with Frank's office, "Frank! You're on shakes tonight!" There was no response. "I know you heard me!" she said as she was halfway to the front.

I asked Terry if he could take me to Mandy's after work. He agreed, for a pack of cigarettes.

♦ ♦ ♦

I stood at the host stand and watched the passers-through pump their gas. I realized that, in my concern about Mandy, I had forgotten all about Kyle and his friends. What if they came back? Would Frank save me again?

A family walked in, looked around without acknowledging me, and then left. Sometimes it was Frank that made them uneasy. Other times I think they just felt the place was beneath them. Mercedes, mostly. Sometimes a Lexus or BMW. They were assigned to Mandy's section if they did stay. I wonder how Carla and Patty treated her in high school, without the veiled protection of Frank? How would they have reacted to her goth look, the acrid smell of cat urine and her trailer park residence? Maybe, to her, I was something more than what I thought I was—and what I've always thought is that I'm nothing.

The teenagers arrived in waves and varying stupidity. How weird, I thought, that only a year ago I was that idiotic, that arrogant. The world hits quick, I guessed. There was a line of nine or ten empty shake glasses. Frank scooped ice cream furiously in his own, awkward way. Sometimes he didn't align the metal cup properly in the machine and milk and strawberries would fly out. It was hypnotic and a train wreck all at once. For several minutes Patty and I watched in a trance. His skinny arms and that see-through white dress shirt.

I heard "Flying chicken!" from behind me as I waited on a table of three middle-school girls who were dropped off by a father. The chicken patty hit me on my back and fell onto the floor. I looked back and saw the boys laughing at their antics.

All three girls had braces, and I couldn't hide my smile when they ordered shakes—one strawberry, one chocolate, and one vanilla. I liked Frank, even before yesterday, but watching him struggle was entertainment I could not pass up. Maybe I'm still an idiot at heart. I slid the chicken patty underneath a booth. Fuck it, and in came Doug, et al.

Patty told me that they wanted me as their waiter. This frightened me. What pamphlet would they leave me with? The one with Jesus or the one with the cross? Perhaps the one that looked like a twenty-dollar bill until you unfold it and *boom* Jesus? At that moment I realized it was Shabbos, how quickly a habit can wilt.

It didn't feel right to piss in Doug's decaf without Mandy by my side. Some couples—are we a couple? Some couples have a shared dance, or a song, or favorite restaurant—we have shared piss.

They said 'please' and 'thank you' a lot. Almost too much. None of them ogled Patty's ass as she served other guests, and when they left there were dollar bills on the table.

"Where does she live?" Terry asked me in his car. He lit a cigarette from the pack I'd bought him in the gas station. I told him over by the Walmart and we headed out. Honestly, that was all I remembered. I'd been there once, in the dark, and I didn't pay close attention. The trailer park had a name. Whispering Pines? Heavenly Pines? Something Pines. If I could get us there, I'd be close enough.

The grease smelled more ingrained on his clothes, more so than mine. Or I had gotten used to it. My feet were in a sea of empty Mountain Dew bottles.

"Frank's always been like that," he said as he blew smoke out the partially open window. "Quiet, but protective, especially with family. I guess he thinks of us as family, 'cept I'm his real family so he'll fight with me. Shit, you got an apron on at that shithole and he'd probably die for you."

I asked him why he was that way, if anything happened to him.

"Not really, just always like that. Was a cop for a few months, but I don't think you can be a quiet guy and be a cop, at least I've never seen that on 'COPS'."

"Would you die for him?" I asked.

He took a drag and flung the butt outside. "I suppose I would, but not like him."

"What do you mean?"

"I mean I probably would, but I don't know. He would. Which street is she on?"

I told him it was a trailer park.

"Hidden Pines, only one over here. I lived in here for a little while. What street?"

I told him I didn't remember, but there was a driveway and wooden steps that led up to the door.

"Every trailer has a driveway and wooden steps."

I told him to look for her car, a Jetta. We couldn't find it, so at Butterfield Lane and

Cinnamon Street he told me to get, he had to get home. The heat from Terry's car left me immediately. I walked down Cinnamon under a full moon and looked for the Jetta, looked in windows for familiarity.

A man walked past an open curtain. Too fat. The shadow of a woman in a bedroom changing. Unknown, but I watched the situation in its entirety. A left down Hickory, a door slammed, and a man's voice said, "Fucking cat piss." I had found her father; I had found her trailer.

♦ ♦ ♦

The late news was on the television. A murdered teenager. A car accident, hit and run, but no one was injured. A landlord shut off the heat and a family froze to death. More snow on the way.

He moved pieces on a chessboard and told me that he was glad to have company at night. That Mandy was at a friend's house. How, if he could afford it, he'd replace the cat litter every day. How he would buy one of the doublewides that were farther from the train tracks. They would have Kentucky Fried Chicken night. Tuesdays, he proffered, and then confirmed. On Wednesdays they would make tacos, and it would be a family event. He would brown the ground beef, his wife would prepare the fixings, and Mandy would warm the tortillas. He asked me if I preferred soft tortillas or hard shells, I told him I enjoyed both kinds. Thursdays would be spaghetti night with *real* garlic bread that you buy in the freezer. Fridays they would get in the car and go out for dinner. Not the gas station restaurant or some fast-food place. No, they'd go to a place with a theme. A Chi-Chi's or a Bennigan's. Where, on Mandy's birthday, they'll make a big show of it with a candle in a piece of cake and they'd all come out from the back singing. And when they brought the check, he'd pull out a wad of bills and tip generously and sit back in his chair with a sated stomach.

January 18

I woke up on their couch under a blanket to the glistening sun filtering through the frosted window and thin shades. Two cats were at my feet, another behind my head. The smell of eggs. Bacon. Her father was at the stove. Her mother drank tea at the table.

He asked me if I drank coffee, then brought me a mug which read 'Delaware, the First State.' I joined her mother at the table and we ate the eggs and bacon. Her mug read, 'Crossroads of America' inside the outline of Indiana and his was from Georgia.

"Sometimes she doesn't come home for days," her mother said.

Her father offered me a ride home and I took it. We didn't speak much, except for when I needed to provide him with directions. "Tell Mandy I'm sorry," I told him before stepping out of the car, "tell her I'm sorry for being a jerk." He nodded affirmatively, then drove off. There was a man sitting in a beach chair smoking a cigarette in front of the room farthest from the motel office. It started to snow.

I picked up the telephone and dialed. My father answered. My car was to be towed to a junkyard. Money would be wired to ship my belongings home, and a plane ticket would be purchased in my name. Grandma had passed away; I had no choice—I had to go home.

January 20

I'd never felt a sense of belonging here, in any synagogue. Inclusion, by its nature, excludes. Why did Moses receive the Ten Commandments in Israel? Why not, say, Beijing? Are the Chinese not Chosen? The Rabbi stood almost motionless on the Bima. I had remembered a more animated man from my Bar Mitzvah. It was the context, I think, rather than the six years that had elapsed since I read from the Torah. Memorized, would be more accurate, as I never understood most of

what I was reading and without the vowels
I'd always been lost.

*Glorified and sanctified be God's great
name throughout the world
which He has created according to His
will.*

*May He establish His kingdom in your
lifetime and during your days,
and within the life of the entire House of
Israel, speedily and soon;
and say, Amen.*

*May His great name be blessed forever
and to all eternity.*

*Blessed and praised, glorified and
exalted, extolled and honored,
adored and lauded be the name of the
Holy One, blessed be He,
beyond all the blessings and hymns,
praises and consolations that
are ever spoken in the world; and say,
Amen.*

*May there be abundant peace from
heaven, and life, for us
and for all Israel; and say, Amen.*

*He who creates peace in His celestial
heights,
may He create peace for us and for all
Israel;
and say, Amen.*

I hid myself behind the dead garden of flowers that lined the stairs to the synagogue entrance and thought about running to the side of the building for a smoke. The doors opened; the sound accentuated by the winter quiet. The pall bearers stepped out and their feet crunched down on the rock salt sprinkled liberally. My father led one side of the casket, followed by my brothers. The other held by cousins and an uncle. A breeze arrived and held, which reminded me of the yarmulke on my head.

We were the last to leave the cemetery. My father stood motionless at the fresh earth pressed down in front of my grandmother's headstone. The undisturbed snow that warmed my grandfather next to her. He tried to hold back, that deep sniffle that lifts one's shoulders that you knew was futile to resist. My brothers approached and put their arms around him. I had never seen him cry before, and I was unsure which headstone was the catalyst.

♦ ♦ ♦

Death is a subdued event surrounded by survivors, I thought. It comes, and is to be expected, like the snow as you stare at the lush leaves in July. Sadness, therefore, is belied for comfort.

No one wept, for to weep is to believe that this circumstance was surprising, and in some spiritual way, avoidable. Sadness was to be conveyed in a dignified fashion.

I avoided eye contact as I walked through my grandmother's house. What would my answers be for my life, and how could they ever compare to my brothers' endeavors? To their own? My cousin, the lawyer, as he whispered the guilt of some poor man in my uncle's ear. The professor on his tenure. The neurosurgeon on call.

No, I focused on the inanimate. The black and white television tucked in the corner, behind the kitchen table. Remembered the lunches of smoked turkey and lettuce on rye bread. A bottle of Dr. Brown's ginger ale. I opened the cabinets and knew which dishes were for meat, and those for dairy. The silver Shabbos candles and how she lit them either out of religious duty or habit. Yiddish for days through the rotary telephone set on an end table between vinyl couches.

I sat down on one nearest the wall and listened to the aged Eastern European accents that bounced off the Midwest American tonal flatness. "Well," my Uncle Anchel said as he sat down next to me with a grunt, "here we are, and we are here." He patted my knee; I hadn't remembered his accent so thick.

"Here we are, Uncle Anchel." My suit was a size too small and I kept pulling my sleeves down. Fuck, I hate wearing a tie. His sleeves were rolled up to the elbows and I could see the faded numbers tattooed on his forearm.

"I feel like, as an old man sitting next to a young man, I should have some wise story to tell you, a young mensch. Especially at a time like this." He paused, and I waited. "Have you eaten, boychik?" I told him I hadn't. "Eat something," and the vinyl couch squeaked as we sat back.

Aunt Esther walked into the room and stood in front of my uncle, who said something to her in Yiddish. "Come, come," she told me, grabbed my hands, and led me to the dining room. In a moment I was holding a plate and she piled it high with deli meats and pickles and bread. She watched me sit down on one of the chairs moved to the wall and only smiled and looked away when I had taken a bite.

How different the Yiddish was from English. For when my grandmother asked me often how school was going, she meant 'knowledge.' To her, it meant I was becoming a better person, one who could contribute something useful. It meant empathy. Growth. The miscommunication was my doing, as I had never found it necessary to learn Yiddish. Or Czech. Or Russian. Perhaps, if I had, then this message would have been clear. Perhaps, had I taken our discussions as more than mere formality, I would have heard her. And as I sat there, trying not to drip pickle juice on my suit pants, I realized that the translation may have been lost on my father's generation as well as mine. I watched them compare university educations, titles and accolades. They were in search of status, each and every one that spoke without an accent. Perhaps it was an overcorrection. Annoying, yes, but something that could be forgiven.

My cousin Eva caught my eye as she crawled on the floor in a flower-print dress. I was jealous that it was socially acceptable for her to remove her shoes. She moved forward along the credenza, followed its corner towards the wall and then appeared through my legs.

"Hi!" she said, giggled, then ran off.

I sat and listened. A paper to be printed in the Harvard Business Review. He was destined to become partner. The rewards of saving a life to one's ego. Animated Yiddish I struggled to understand. That, I thought, is a story worth hearing. Plans laid out for each phase of life. A plan for childbirth. For promotions. The best investments. The general cost increase of a college education in year X and how to match said investments with the estimated birth date of child number one, number two, and a contingency plan for a third. Real estate best practices and the three key points to operating a successful business as told by David. How his introduction to yoga by his beloved wife Miriam has reduced his stress levels. A new understanding of the stock market as relayed by my brother. A recounting of baseball triumphs and sacrilegious comparisons to Sandy Koufax. His grades, someone chimed, were the real triumphs.

It was so brave of him to forgo athletic achievement for a more noble purpose. Yes, they joked, the Mercedes and five-bedroom house were nice perks, but only a side-effect of standing up for science, for pharma.

I went to the kitchen, shook the food I hadn't eaten into the waste bin and placed my plate in the sink. Grabbed my coat. Left through the side door and lit a cigarette at the driveway's end. Looked inside the window and the conversations were much more palatably muted. Eva climbed up on the couch and waved. I walked to the neighbor's driveway, stopped, and looked at the window again. It began to snow.

At some point, still within the neighborhood, I had decided to run—although I couldn't pinpoint exactly when. Through traffic stopped at red lights. A pharmacy parking lot. Down strip mall walkways. Across streets in complete disobedience to 'don't walk' indicators. Adjacent to highway on-ramps and related off-ramps.

I turned the front door handle and the motion stopped. Locked. Punched in the code for the garage door and waited with short breath. Pushed the numbers again. *Enter.* Nothing. Once more. *Enter.* Ran around to the backyard, pushed the table up against the brick wall and climbed up onto the foot of accumulated snow to the kitchen window. Slid the right window left, which was enough room to reach my arm inside and remove the lock. Pulled my arm out, slid the left window right and fell into the house behind the table. I lifted myself up and stayed eye level with the car keys for a second.

Pushed aside the socks set in neat rows. Opened an envelope and shoved twenty-dollar bills into my pocket. Closed my father's dresser. I went to my room and took the guitar case and a duffel bag; the rest of my belongings were somewhere between here and Nebraska. Bounded down the stairs, grabbed the car keys, turned for the front door and stopped. "Aaron," I wrote on the back of an envelope where his keys had been, "I borrowed your car. Sandy."

I drove with speed, first and foremost. Easing off the gas only when Aaron's radar detector chirped. I'd never been in the car when he'd sped, so I never understood his need for the device. I made a promise to myself to only stop for gas, and only then was I allowed to piss. Maybe smoke. The traffic eased, the road opened up, and I put the thought of my brother calling the police aside. I was going west. Again.

◆ ◆ ◆

A child ran ahead of his mother and father in the dark parking lot. He grunted as he tried to open the door, but it was too heavy for his small frame. "C'mon, Mama! Papa! It's cold!" They lumbered forward; their large frames made them sway in slow motion. The father pulled the door open and the child went inside. Mandy waited until they were static near the host stand before smiling. Three menus in hand, they followed her into the smoking section.

I wondered how she would greet me. She'd have to meet me out here, as I had a better idea of how the others would greet me—as a traitor, as someone who simply disappeared. Someone who made someone else's job harder, if only for a shift or two. Who was just like the others who couldn't handle Frank, the shit tips, and the smell of walk-in sex. Reason, I think, works best with those who know context, and I'd given them nothing to build upon. Time to get out of the car and stare at her until she felt it.

January 23

I woke up on a bed under a blanket to the biting sun filtering through the frosted window and thin shades. The smell of industrial cleanser made me gasp and I sat up. Felt the agony of my ribs, that gripping pain where you consider not taking another breath just to alleviate the sharpness. A locomotive versus pedestrian in five-second intervals.

My jaw was swollen. A sting underneath my eye. I tried to stand but it felt as if there was a weight embedded between my brain and the back of my skull. The needle embedded in my forearm. Fluids in sterile plastic bags. Garbled voices through ceiling speakers. Beeps and tones. I fell back on to the pillow and breathed.

I remembered Kyle in his 'I'm Kyle' work shirt walking towards me in the parking lot. He said something, "Hey, what's up?" or "What up, dog?" He was smoking a cigarette. He smiled. A sharp pain that ended quickly and then nothing.

"And how are we this morning, Sandy?" the nurse asked me as she entered the room.

"Sandy?"

"Yes, unless we're more formal this morning and you've changed your mind."

"No, Sandy is fine."

She inspected my eye, my jaw, and exposed my thigh covered with a purplish-red bruise. "Soon enough, you'll be out of here."

I wanted to ask her how long I'd been there, but I didn't want to sound dumb.

"Your girlfriend told me to tell you that she'll be by this morning."

"My girlfriend?"

"Yes, you had fallen asleep before she left yesterday."

How long had I been here? A day, a week, a month? Was I smoother with the ladies drugged up and half-comatose?

"You'll be out of here soon enough, then you two can continue on." She wrote something on a clipboard. "I hope someday I see your name on a screen."

"What?"

"You're going to Los Angeles." I didn't understand. "You're going to Los Angeles to be a famous movie director."

"I am?" I paused to ponder how she knew that. "I am."

She smiled and left the room. How many conversations had I had with her since I arrived? What had I said? I took comfort that, whatever I'd said, so far it all made sense.

I woke when I felt a hand clasp mine. My vision cleared and I saw Mandy standing over the bed. "So, you're my girlfriend now?"

"I asked you to be my boyfriend and you said yes."

"I did?"

"Well, you were half-dead, but it counts."

She told me that two plow drivers pulled up as Kyle and his friends were beating on me. They scared them off with shovels and that intensity found only in middle-aged men with children. One came into the restaurant and screamed for help while the other tended to me. "You were in a bad way. Frank called 911 and then ran outside. There was blood flowing from your mouth and my nose. Frank kept saying 'stay with me, son, stay with me.' He said he could see fear in your eyes, that fear that comes when death is close. You were in a bad way. Terry ran all over the parking lot looking for them. A man possessed, I thought at the time. The ambulance came and they put you on a stretcher and I rode with you to the hospital. They thought I was your girlfriend. I mean, technically I was at that point, and they asked me if I could handle the honest truth. I said I could, and they said that you might not make it."

I told her I'd always thought I'd die getting shot. "By who?" I didn't know. She squeezed my hand. "If you don't remember any of this tomorrow, I'll understand." I told her I promise to remember. She smiled, took my hand and kissed it gently.

"I have to go," she told me, "Frank gets worried if I'm not on time for my shift."

"He worries about you *now*?"

"No, he worries about *you*."

January 25

10° outside. I can't get this room warm. I put a towel against the bottom of the door to stop the frigid wind. The heater makes this clicking noise so it should work. I guess it kind of works. The comforters have this weird smell, like mildew and body odor. The faucets run brown with rust for several minutes. Everything I own is in a duffel bag and a guitar case.

Mandy had me write down every phone number she could possibly reach me at and my parent's address. I handed her the piece of paper, she folded it neatly and slid it into her back pocket. I picked up the phone and dialed.

"Darsh, it's Sandy."

"How's Hollywood, brother?"

"Haven't made it there yet. Got jumped."

"By who?"

"Anti-Semites."

"Nazi cocksuckers. I fucking hate them."

"I need the 'Brown Tornado'."

"Where?"

"Nebraska. Look up the Comfort Lane Motel. I-80 West. Exit 49. You'll see a restaurant attached to a gas station. Turn right, you'll see it."

"Be there tomorrow."

"Who you bringing?"

"The fucking United Nations."

"Word."

"See you tomorrow."

I hung up the receiver and turned my head towards Mandy. She unzipped her hoodie to reveal her breasts. "Are you up for it?" I told her I couldn't resist it if I tried. She took a swig of whiskey and handed the bottle to me. I washed down the stale remnants of opiates to quiet the new noise in my head and pushed her down on the bed.

January 26

It was difficult to have secrets in a small town. Couple that with a lack of places to go, and it was hard to hide. Routine was amplified and easy to decode. Saturday night meant billiards at Pete's, an all-ages venue two miles south from the Walmart. I reversed my brother's car into a parking space a ways off from the entrance, darkened where the floodlight couldn't quite reach. Darsh did the same and parked next to me. I took a seat on the trunk of Aaron's car, lit a cigarette for Mandy and one for myself.

"You sure they don't have guns?" I asked her again.

"Never seen them with any guns."

"We don't have guns," I said with a tinge of worry.

"Well, then maybe your worry will come true then."

"I didn't say I wanted to get shot, I said I thought I'd get shot."

"Fate doesn't care about what you want."

The windows were fogged from the body heat inside and the cold external air. We assumed they were inside. Kyle's truck was parked, but we weren't completely sure. How terrible I would have felt had Darsh and my friends driven such a distance for an anticlimactic evening in a pool hall parking lot.

I looked at Darsh's car and watched the cigarette smoke roll out from partially open windows, tinted to hide their figures. Made a fist to test the balance of painkillers and adrenaline, it seemed right. A group of teenage girls in tank tops and skirts walked fast from the door to a car, passed around a bottle, then ran back inside. Two boys hustled to the dark and a lighter flicked. The smoke wafted our way and made us jealous.

It was the anger placed on the door as it flung open that made me think it was them. That always-on mentality of the male adolescent that drains him in his thirties and kills him off by 47. Each day between that produced poor decisions corrected by cheap, cold beer in cans designed to alleviate the regret of bruises on a woman's face and a child's arms. His ribs. Her torso, until his heart gives out or his truck flips on an icy overpass. I exhaled. Flicked my cigarette. Cleared my throat and reassured my own insane, dark heart.

"What's up, Kyle?"

"Look at this, this Jew, he's back for more!"

"Thought you were dead!" his friend yelled.

"Jews don't die!"

"Yeah, I know about six million of them that would say otherwise! Oh, wait, they can't!"

"Shoulda put him in an oven!" another friend screamed.

Darsh opened his car door and stepped out like a fucking 80s action star getting titled up with the camera.

"Oh look, you brought a nig..." he paused, considered that *that* word might invoke a rage that he could not control. Perhaps he had seen *Birth of a Nation* as a foundation for his hatred and did not want to see the wide-eyed, crazed 'negro' portrayed by white men in blackface on Darsh's face. "You brought a Black guy with you, can't fight your own fight?"

"Getting jumped by a bunch of guys is fair?!"

"I'm Indian, you dumb fuck!"

Kyle pushed his head forward and squinted. "Well, it's still four against two, unless your little Jew-loving girlfriend is gonna fight for you."

Darsh knocked twice on his car window. Marcus, Jacob, and Teddy appeared, and all five of us took our line in front of the cars.

"Filipino!" Marcus yelled, "Case you want to figure out how you hate me."

"WASP! White Anglo Saxon Protestant, figure out what the fuck to do with that you piece of shit." Jacob spit towards Kyle.

"A fucking Asian," Teddy felt obliged to say, as he was next in the line, "figure out which kind and I'll buy you a fucking cookie!"

"And I'm a fucking Jew!" I screamed and started walking towards them. Proof that those pills provided, if not invincibility, a sense of impending accomplishment. I could smell the whiskey courage on my friends' breath.

Kyle backed up a step, saw that it elicited doubt among his friends, and moved forward. Marcus had no time for indecision and tackled the boy next to Kyle. He sat on his chest and, with his left hand, held the boy's head a few inches from the gravel before bringing down the right. Then again, and once more, until there was a pool of crimson evidence and his eyes lost focus. I swung at Kyle's friend, missed, and he landed a fist across my jaw. I hunched over for the pain and waited, but it didn't come. I stood up and let him punch me again, smiled, grabbed behind his head and brought my knee to his ribs. As he keeled over, I pulled his body down to the ground and ran his face against the rocks. I rose, drove my shin into his ribs and liver. Just as my foot lined up to kick through his head, someone pulled me off. Kyle had my shoulders and I saw his head approach in slow motion. I reeled backwards, reminded myself of immortality, ducked under his punch, and took him to the ground with a double leg takedown. I pulled myself up his body and set my shin against his neck to watch him struggle for each breath. I watched his defense wilt, his hands fell from my face, and at that point I released. He gasped to regain oxygen and I placed my boot on his cheek. Pushed my toe into his left eye while I stared at the right. I heard Darsh yell that it was time to go and saw Marcus get into Darsh's car. A crowd had formed at the pool hall entrance. I lifted my foot, thought about stomping down Kyle's face, then stepped over and got into my brother's car with Mandy. I didn't see what Marcus or Teddy did, but the aftermath made me think something horrible.

We stopped at the gas station attached to the restaurant for cigarettes and supplies. I gave each of my friends a hug with the obligatory two pats on the back. I thanked them and they insisted it wasn't necessary. I veered right at the junction to head west, they continued a quarter mile and veered left. I felt vindicated, and that now was an appropriate time to forgive Kyle. To forget him. I was going to Los Angeles to be a famous film director with my girl at my side.

◆ ◆ ◆

"I want to hear it," she said.
"I've never said it before."
"No better time than now."
"I mean, I think it."

"About me?"

"Of course, who else?"

"I don't know."

"Okay, I'll say it."

"No."

"What?"

"I only want you to say it if you want to say it."

"I do want to say it."

"But I don't want you to say it when I ask, I want it to be, you know, spontaneous."

"But you already know I'm going to say it."

"Still. Don't say it."

We had changed our route west based on the advice of an elderly man with a long gray beard who was eating pancakes. It was the way he ate that caused me to finally say something to him after so many discreet glances that he probably felt. Softened with melted butter and doused in syrup, slurped down and perhaps he had some teeth way back in his mouth but I wasn't sure.

I asked him how the pancakes were and he said "Fine, fine. Fine pancakes here." He slurped his coffee the same as the pancakes. I told him that I can't eat pancakes without a glass of milk. "Some peoples like that, I guess."

Mandy kicked my shin to get me to disengage with him. She told me later that she found him creepy. I told him that we're heading out west. "Gonna dig up some gold?" I told him I didn't understand. "Gonna go find your fortune? That's the reason to go out west." Yes, I thought, in a way. "You two Romeos and Juliets? Run away to be in love?"

The waitress put her hand on his shoulder when she refilled his mug. He looked up at her and smiled while keeping his lips pursed. She mirrored him, aware, I thought, that her full set of teeth would cause him pain, or discomfort at the least. I wondered if the cook was anything like Terry. He was a large man, Black, and practically roared when he laughed. I couldn't imagine him fornicating with a young woman in a walk-in.

The elderly man told us that we'd have to wait it out if we wanted to continue through the mountains. Snowstorms coming through, he said, before correctly assuming that our car didn't have snow tires. "Probably not tuned for the altitude," he added. I imagined him panning for gold in the hot sun and playing sad bluegrass on his old guitar at a campfire alone with the stars. "In my younger days, I could make all the girls dance," he said to his pancakes. "Had me lined up any Juliet. Got older and they called me 'Black Wolf' and got older and it's what you see." He put his arms out and swung his body slowly, scanning the restaurant, "No Juliets here for me." He set a pile of single dollar bills on the table and left.

"I think you're more like my Bonnie and I'm Clyde," I told Mandy.

"I'm your Mandy, and you're my Sanford."

"Not your Sandy?"

"No, we're too far gone for nicknames, hyphenations, or altered spellings."

I had a thought that her full name was Miranda, but I didn't want to end our meal with an awkward inconsistency debated for no reason.

January 27/28

Our directions were printed on a diner napkin with blue ink as dictated by an elderly man with a gray beard who slurped down pancakes. A man without teeth is a man who has lived, there was no reason to doubt his advice.

I took the first shift as driver and cut southwest through Kansas and Colorado. Wove around semi-trucks and sedans and SUVs in the American darkness, deep within the interior. To me, there was a nothingness save tarmac and green metal signs with reflective white words. Numbers. Arrows. I felt ultra-sober with the wheel, the crackly replays of church services on AM radio. Content with the soft snores from my passenger. Alive when I rolled the window down an inch and felt the cold air rush in across my forehead. The lighter as it illuminated in my near vision and the smoke as it sped to the open window. That freedom when all the crimson tail lights disappear and the yellow din of approaching vehicles follows suit. It was pure in the dashboard's glow and the hum of tires against the road—that soft roar against the undercarriage.

We ate McMuffins in an Albuquerque McDonald's parking lot. Felt the warmth of 45° with the windows wide and imagined the lives as each car pulled up to the speaker. There was a minivan with a woman and three children who appeared and then hid in the dark spaces. A man in flannel with his dog. A woman in a business suit who alternated between applying mascara and smoking a cigarette. Six teenagers stuffed into a hatchback. We watched an aged couple plod slowly to the door without a care for the drive-thru traffic they were holding back. I crumpled the McMuffin wrapper and there, in that McDonald's parking lot in Albuquerque, New Mexico, I understood America. We were free to continue west, and as Mandy shifted into drive, I rested my head against the seat and closed my eyes.

A sparsely treed landscape upon a tan world greeted me under a strong sun. I rolled the window down and extended my arm as far as possible. Felt the wind against my skin and breathed in the desert air, maybe 60° but a perfect 72 in my mind.

Mandy pulled over and we walked a hundred yards from the highway. I took in the mesas and the bluffs and dug lines into the beige dirt with the tip of my shoe. Inspected the brownish-green shrubs that looked so alien to my midwestern experience. She put her arm around my waist and pulled me to her. "We'll be there tonight," she said quietly, almost in a whisper.

It was understood that I would take the wheel for the final leg. That I would bring us into Los Angeles proper and deliver us into our next lives. The desert in front of us was fated to be behind us. Only hours. Only hours. Freedom from winter wrapped in a celluloid dream. set my foot on the gas pedal, the gravel of the highway shoulder flew backwards, and I watched the insignificant pebbles fall harmlessly to the pavement. Each had a name, and each was back there, somewhere, and they won't ever find me.

♦ ♦ ♦

I parked my brother's car along a street and tried not to think about our funds and what must be done in the near term to compensate. Those thoughts go dormant on a mission. We walked north on Cahuenga Boulevard with the slow, gawking characteristics distinctive of Hollywood tourists.

An obese woman appeared from the shadows and approached. She looked like a prostitute who hadn't changed her risqué attire in weeks. Lipstick melded to her lips, thick and the darkest red. Black fishnet stockings where the diamond patterns were clinging on in only a few places and ran under her cracked leather skirt. Mandy grasped my hand tight, later revealing that she was preparing herself to see a veiny breast and large areola pop out and attack her in some fashion. Her male companion walked alongside her. Equally fat, his stained white t-shirt and stained brown blue jeans and caked mud steel-toe boots. She stopped when she saw us and he took one extra step before halting himself. Ten feet separated us, maybe eight. He belched and I think he threw up a little in his mouth then swallowed. She lifted her skirt several inches to where we could see the overflow of fat on her thighs, then squatted on the sidewalk. Mandy squeezed my hand like I assume a wife does to her husband when she is in labor as the woman urinated on the pavement. Her face contorted, as if it didn't come naturally or provide relief. She must have sensed the horror in Mandy's eyes, as she smiled wide and lifted her hips so the spray would come closer.

We were frozen, we wanted to run but couldn't find our feet. The man coughed and then spit phlegm into her puddle of piss. She shimmied her panties with a series of grunts until they disappeared under her skirt. We watched the couple walk into the traffic to scream at drivers who dared to honk their horns.

We walked upon the stars embedded in the sidewalks and I thought about my name engraved. Those magnificent faces that glow on television screens and in movie theaters. So important that they are chased by photographers and men with microphones to keep tabs on their every move. I vowed, at that moment, that I would remain grounded when they chased me. That they would still be my peers, and that I would not let my ego run amok.

Every now and again we'd see an exotic car, a Lamborghini or Ferrari. Hear the loud bass from a Mercedes with windows tinted black. See who we thought was a celebrity and then backtrack after further consideration. We dared not enter the bars as we didn't know how we would be received upon ordering an adult beverage.

In the passenger seat there was the sudden realization that maybe, just maybe, I had no idea what to do next. I lit a cigarette to erase the thought and it remained. Mandy pulled into a Jack in the Box parking lot. "I have to pee, and I'm hungry."

Someone had carved the anarchy symbol into the tile above the urinal. A smiley face and an erect cock. "Max is gay. Ketchup is mustard. Screenwriter's blues. Suck my cock." The word made my mind run as if I was on acid. Was I Max? Am I gay? How high does this ketchup/mustard conspiracy go? The CIA? The president? Oh shit, now I know, and they know I know. Am I a screenwriter or a director? Am I sad? No, I'm not Max, but I have to suck his cock. Wait, am I gay? Do they let gay Jews become film directors here? Am

I Jewish? What is Jack in the Box? *Who* is Jack? *What* is Jack? Who put him in a box? Fuck, I'm hungry now.

♦ ♦ ♦

60° outside. I'm sitting at the small motel table and blowing cigarette smoke out the open window. When the light breeze swirls and flows inside its coolness is warm to my midwestern expectations. There's a dust everywhere it can settle, like the windowsill, as if it's taunting rain. I'm jealous that it's never seen snow, felt the sting of horizontal sleet smacking its face. I have this nervous energy, perhaps too excited for the morning, the warmth of the California sun. I had made it. *We* had made it.

January 29

They came just before daylight. Steady knocks on the motel door. One. Two. Three. I thought I was dreaming. I heard Mandy stir, I think. They knocked again. One. Two. Three. Mandy pushed on my shoulder, I slipped out of the bed and walked the few steps to the door. In my slumbering mind I didn't think to ask who was there, I just turned the knob. They were yelling things as they pushed inside, none of which I could comprehend. The swiftness of their entry whipped the winter wind and I felt a chill across my naked chest. In my peripheral, I saw Mandy push herself up against the headboard, she held the comforter over her body. I felt metal against my back, everything that touched me was intolerably cold. My shoulder popped as a hand grasped my wrist and pulled it behind my back. Lucidity came in waves. The Nazis had told the cops. My other shoulder strained. We had killed one of them. A boot against the back of my knee dropped me to the floor. They were getting Darsh as we spoke, and I was the one who got him into this. One of them took my wallet from my jeans and inspected my driver's license. Another sat me down on a chair, hard.

I wanted to look away from Mandy, from her frightened eyes. I wanted to apologize and tell them she had nothing to do with any of this. That it was all me. No words came, I just stared at her pressed against the headboard, unsure of what comes next. I listened to the squawking voices coming through the radios pinned to their shoulders. A hand grabbed my arm and lifted my body. "I love you," I said, quietly and with a crackled voice. Mandy didn't respond. "I love you!" I shouted, which took them by surprise.

"I love you, too," she whispered and smiled. William H. Parker, as denoted by his metal tag, checked my coat pockets then flung it over my shoulders and led me out to their waiting car.

January 31

The plan, as I'd been told, was to teach me a lesson about 'responsibility.' About 'consequences.' To correct their meandering nomad in a desert of nothingness, surviving on manna far from the Holy Land. Perhaps all of this empty talk of success and fame could be overlooked had the boy an ounce of charisma, even the semblance of charm. I was an error, a glitch in the family program. Maybe that was a tad harsh, it was hard to be optimistic in a holding cell.

My brother would report his car as stolen—by me, and they would arrest me and this would scare me into reevaluating my life. Once this epiphany had been realized, vocalized, the charges were to be dropped and I would enroll in a university and become a respected member of society. Everything had been arranged. The rabbi had been consulted. The psychologist had provided his guidance. The prosecutor promised the result, should I have this awakening. The defense attorney provided the plan's second opinion and his blessing. What they had failed to consider, however, was that I was wanted for questioning for an assault in Nebraska.

February 7

The prosecutor called it understandable, given what had happened to me and he read aloud the injuries that had been written on my hospital chart. Yet, he contended that the proper thing that I should have done, the *legal* course of action, would have been to file a police report. According to him, I had organized my gang of thugs in a premeditated attack on young men who may or may not have attacked me. They were good boys, just a little rough around the edges.

I could hear my mother's sniffles in a chair behind me and summoned the courage to turn my neck. She stared at the floor and discretely wiped her tears with a tissue half hidden in her fist. Shabbos would begin in a few hours, I wondered if she had thought about the candles. I thought about the bland food in the jail and salivated to the aroma of brisket and potatoes. How the challah felt so delicate. That grape sweetness not found in the gentile world.

How my father's features would differ in this courtroom had I been that prosecutor. That defense attorney. How he would beam if I were called as an expert witness. What proud stories he would tell at the next funeral, where there was one less Yiddish voice with faded numbers embedded in wrinkled skin. What proud stories *I* would tell, of successful surgeries and neurological breakthroughs. Journal publications and thought-leadership pieces on large stages at annual conventions.

I wrote on the legal pad in front of me—I am going to Los Angeles to be a film director. I am going to tell stories about lovers and spies and dystopian futures. To make love to actresses and watch my bank account grow exponentially until my Jewish American Princess files for divorce. Then I'll be free to make love to models half my age. I am going to Los Angeles.

Other books by Steven W. Simon

Into the Fracking Fields | A Novel

The kids in the border town watch the prisoners get off the trains and load up on the bus. Alice has heard the rumors of the people who stayed, their proximity to Nuclear One, their cancerous lumps. Her friend Carmen is driven to see the fracking pad where his father was killed – and Michael, unfortunately, is the only one that can get them there.

Red as Apple | A Novella

It has been years since Keenan had been to the farm. He had vowed to move on, to move up, but this has brought him back. To his introverted older brother and confident sister. After this, their lives will never be the same.

Out Pondered the Hare | Poems

A collection of poems written in sobriety. Or a Lorazepam fog. A whiskey-infused detour and lysergic-stamped synapses - much of which is about my teenage years in Metro Detroit. All in the hopes that some of this makes sense to those who were not there in those specific instances where there is truth.

boundharepress.com

www.ingramcontent.com/pod-product-compliance
Lightning Source LLC
Chambersburg PA
CBHW030324160726
47992CB00005B/2147